Science ~~Action Labs~~

Water Science

PARENT-TEACHER COLLECTION

Written by Ed Shevick

Illustrated by Mary Galan Rojas

Teaching & Learning Company

1204 Buchanan St., P.O. Box 10
Carthage, IL 62321-0010

This book belongs to

Cover art by Mary Galan Rojas

Copyright © 2002, Teaching & Learning Company

ISBN No. 1-57310-364-0

Printing No. 987654321

Teaching & Learning Company
1204 Buchanan St., P.O. Box 10
Carthage, IL 62321-0010

Table of Contents
Science Action Labs

1: Wonderful Water 5

2: Three Kinds of Water 9

3: Water Dissolves 15

4: Water Evaporates 18

5: Water Pressure 23

6: Water Has a Skin 27

7: More About Water's Skin 31

8: Water Puzzlers 34

9: Floating on Water 37

10: Water and Your Body 43

11: Water and Plants.............................47

12: The Water Cycle 52

13: Protecting and Saving Water 56

14: Frozen Water 61

Answer Key 64

LC10364 Copyright © Teaching & Learning Company, Carthage, IL 62321-0010

Dear Teacher or Parent,

Welcome to *Science Action Labs: Water Science*. This book is built around solid scientific concepts which are backed up by basic facts. The concepts are made real by meaningful activities and experiments designed to interest and motivate your children. Each one involves some part of the scientific process. All activities are not suitable for every age or ability. This gives the teacher an opportunity to pick and choose for particular children.

Since the concepts build on one another, proceed from lab 1 onward. However, each chapter can stand on its own as an independent lab if you choose to teach them in a different order.

Sometimes it may be best to do the activities as demonstrations instead of lab activities. Questions are provided for group discussions.

Above all, children should be allowed to enjoy science. Fun and excitement are inherent in the process of discovery. To make the fact-finding activities in this study more fun, meet C.D. (collecting data), his ally Allie and her cat Orbit. They'll help children gather and process information and encourage them as only kids can do.

Sincerely,

Ed

Ed Shevick

Wonderful Water

Water Science 1

The Wonders of Water

Water covers $3/4$ of the Earth's surface. It is the liquid we drink, it is in the ice we skate on and it is in the steam from a boiling teakettle.

Water is a part of all living things. Over $2/3$ of your body is water. If you weigh 90 pounds, you contain 60 pounds of water.

List 10 ways you and your family use water.

1. _____

2. _____

3. _____

4. _____

5. _____

6. _____

7. _____

8. _____

9. _____

10. _____

Wonderful Water

A Close Look at Water

1. Fill a glass with water and look at it closely.

2. Look through a glass of water. Can you see beyond the glass? Light goes right through water. What color is the water in the glass? Does it seem colorless? It is. Water in oceans sometimes seems to be green or blue because of the sunlight and the depth of the water.

3. Dip your finger into the glass. Is it easy to push the water aside? That is because this water is in a liquid state.

4. Dip your finger in and out of the water and raise it into the air. Does your finger feel cool? The water is evaporating into the air. Evaporation cools things.

5. Taste some fresh, clean water. Can you describe the taste? That isn't easy because pure water is tasteless.

6. Pour a little salt or sugar into a glass of water. Stir it up. Can you see the salt? Some things dissolve in water and seem to disappear.

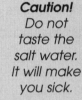

Caution! *Do not taste the salt water. It will make you sick.*

Name _____

Wonderful Water

A Close Look at Water Drops

1. Turn on your faucet. The water comes out in a steady stream.

2. Slowly turn the faucet off until you get a series of small drops. Observe the drops at eye level. What is their shape when they first come out? What is their shape as they fall?

3. Find an eyedropper or dropper bottle. Place a water drop on a paper towel. What happens to the water?

4. Place a drop on a piece of plastic. What happens to the drop? Does it have a particular shape?

5. Let some drops fall into a glass of water. Look right at water level. Describe what you observe.

The Quarter Water Challenge

Compete with your friends on this experiment. Place a white card under a quarter. Slowly add drops of water on top of the quarter. Count the drops until you see water overflowing on the card.

I had 10 drops. Can you do more? Notice how the water bulges above the quarter. Water acts as if it has a skin.

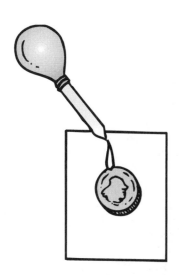

Review Quiz

1. What is frozen water called? _____

2. What comes out of a boiling teakettle? _____

3. If you drink about 2$\frac{1}{2}$ quarts of water each day, how many quarts would

   you drink in four days? _____

4. Ninety-seven percent of the Earth's water is salty. What percent is left that

   is fresh water? _____

5. What would your life be like without water? Write at least three complete

   sentences to answer the question. _____

   _____

   _____

   _____

   _____

   _____

   _____

Three Kinds of Water

Water Is Different

Water is special. Water is the only substance that exists on Earth in three forms: liquid, solid (ice) and gas (steam).

Experiment

Let's change water from a solid to a liquid to a gas.

1. Place four ice cubes in a teakettle.
2. Place the kettle on a stove and have an adult turn it on. What will happen to the ice?
3. Keep heating the water that develops from the ice. What happens to the water?

When water is a solid (ice) it has a definite shape. As a liquid, water takes on the shape of its container. **Steam** is water in the form of gas.

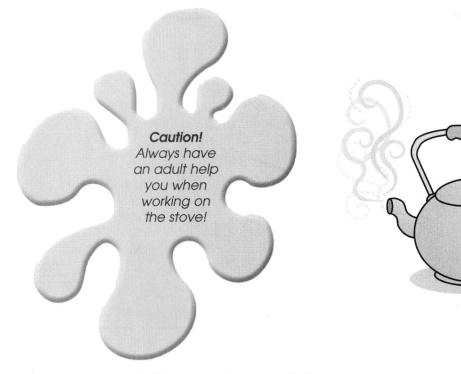

Caution!
Always have an adult help you when working on the stove!

The Water Molecule

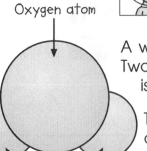

Oxygen atom

Hydrogen atoms

A water molecule is made up of three atoms. Two of the atoms are **hydrogen**. The third atom is **oxygen**.

The three atoms are joined together to form a water molecule which is much too small for us to see. Trillions of water molecules would fit in a teaspoon.

No one has "seen" a water molecule, but scientists believe they look something like the sketch to the left: a large oxygen atom with two smaller hydrogen atoms attached.

Just like us—The Three Musketeers!

Imagination Time
Scientists call water H_2O (two Hydrogen atoms and one Oxygen). Imagine that you have seen a water molecule. Draw what you think it might look like in the box. Be creative and even humorous.

Name _____

Three Kinds of Water

Water Molecules in Motion

Think of a glass of water. It has trillions of molecules. Water molecules never stay still. They are constantly moving and bumping into each other. It is like a molecular dance.

Water molecules dance because of heat. Cold molecules move slowly. Hot molecules move faster.

Experiment

1. Fill a glass $3/4$ full of cold water.

2. Fill another glass $3/4$ full of very warm water. Both should be filled to the same height.

3. Quickly add two drops of a dark vegetable dye to both glasses of water. Don't stir or move the glasses.

4. Watch as the dye spreads throughout the water. In which glass did the dye spread faster?

Remember that hot molecules move faster than cold molecules. Use this fact to explain what happened in each glass.

> Here is an experiment to let you observe water molecules dancing.

Three Kinds of Water

Human Water Molecules

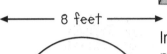

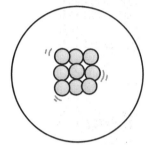

Ice molecules

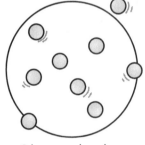

Water molecules

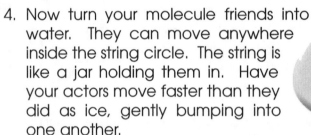

Steam molecules

Imagine that you have been made director of a water molecule play. Find nine friends to act as molecules.

1. Use string to mark off an eight-foot circle.

2. Line up your molecule friends to form a square in the center of the circle as shown.

3. They are now molecules of ice. Have them gently bump into one another. Even ice molecules are in motion.

4. Now turn your molecule friends into water. They can move anywhere inside the string circle. The string is like a jar holding them in. Have your actors move faster than they did as ice, gently bumping into one another.

5. Move your molecules even faster to be steam. A few should move outside the string. They are gas now and are free to escape anywhere.

If it is a nice day, you can do this activity outside!

Three Kinds of Water

Key Word Review

Complete the following statements with the key words below.

fast
slow
escape
moving
shape
container

1. Water molecules are always _____.

2. Hot water molecules move _____.

3. Cold water molecules move _____.

4. Water in the form of ice has a definite _____.

5. Liquid water takes the shape of its _____.

6. Steam molecules can _____ into the air.

13

Water Poetry

Use any of these words to write a short poem about water.

solid
liquid
gas
hydrogen
oxygen

_____

_____

_____

_____

_____

_____

_____

Water Dissolves

Water Science

3

Will It or Won't It Dissolve?

Ocean water tastes salty because salt has dissolved in it. You can't see the dissolved salt but you could taste it.

Experiment

Caution! *Do not drink salt water.*

Water dissolves many common substances. Let's experiment with common household items. Which will dissolve in water?

Fill a shallow bowl with water. Change the water as needed.

Try items such as salt, pepper, tea, rice, flour, spices and whatever is available. List your results below.

Water Dissolves It	Water Does Not Dissolve It
1.	1.
2.	2.
3.	3.
4.	4.
5.	5.
6.	6.

Water Dissolves

The Space in Water

If you add sugar to water it dissolves and seems to disappear. You can't see it. Where did it go?

Experiment

Here is an experiment that helps explain where the sugar went.

1. Fill a glass $2/3$ full of water.

2. Place a rubber band around the glass at the water level.

3. Add four level teaspoons of sugar to the water and stir it with a spoon.

4. Check the water level. Did it go up above the rubber band mark? Where do you think the sugar is?

Water molecules move around. To move, there must be space between the molecules.

Water molecules only

The missing sugar molecules must be in those spaces.

Water and
sugar molecules

Water Dissolves

Not Everything Dissolves in Water

Sugar dissolves in water; other substances do not. Here is a liquid to experiment with. Will this liquid find a home between water molecules?

Tight Lid

Oil

Water

Experiment

1. Fill a small jar with a tight lid half full of water.

2. Pour $\frac{1}{2}$" of cooking oil into the jar. Did the oil dissolve in the water? Describe what happened.

3. Secure the lid very tightly on the jar. Shake up the oil and water vigorously.

4. Let the jar stand for a few minutes. Describe what happened. Does oil dissolve in water?

I tried the oil and water experiment. I was curious. I heard that soap breaks up oil. I added 10 to 15 drops of liquid soap to the oil and water mixture. Then I shook the jar vigorously.

Try C.D.'s experiment for yourself.

17

Water Science 4

Water Evaporates

What Causes Evaporation?

Water falls from clouds. Gravity pulls the raindrops down to Earth.

How does rain get back into the clouds? The answer is **evaporation**.

Pulling water up against gravity takes energy. The sun provides this energy. The sun heats up water so that some escapes as a gas. The light gas molecules drift upward to join clouds.

Water evaporates from oceans, lakes and even wet sidewalks.

Experiment

Let's use the sun's energy to evaporate water.

1. On a warm, sunny day, place two equal-sized small saucers upside down in the sunlight.
2. Put a teaspoon of water on the top of each saucer.
3. Cover one saucer with a glass. Leave the other uncovered.
4. Wait 20 to 30 minutes.

What happened to the water in the uncovered saucer?

Where did the water go?

What gave the water molecules the energy to leave?

What do you see in the covered saucer?

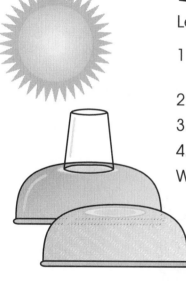

Name _____

Another Sun Experiment

How much water can evaporate in a few hours? Here is how to find out.

1. Fill a wide-mouth jar $3/4$ full of water.

2. Put a rubber band around the jar to mark the water level.

3. Put the jar outside in the bright sun. This may take more than one day. If so, take the jar in at night.

4. Look at the water level in the jar. Has it gone down? Measure how far it went down in inches and write it here.

_____ inches

Your jar is just a tiny example of the surfaces on Earth where water is evaporating all the time.

Scientists estimate that the sun's energy evaporates a trillion tons of water every day!

Water Evaporates

 ## The Salty Ocean

The ocean is salty. Does the salt in the ocean evaporate with the water? Let's find out.

Experiment

1. Mix two level teaspoons of salt in a $\frac{1}{4}$ glass of water. Stir it with a spoon until you can't see the salt.

2. Pour a thin layer of the water into a shallow saucer.

3. Place it in the bright sun for two to four hours. When the water evaporates, what do you see in the saucer?

Stir it with a spoon till you can't see the salt.

Have you ever been swimming in the ocean? After you sat in the sun, did your skin feel crusty? That was salt from the water.

That's nothing! Try dipping your paw in the Great Salt Lake!

20

Water Evaporates

Evaporation Art

Would you like to be an evaporation artist? Here is a way to draw with the sun as your helper.

1. Mix a dark vegetable dye or liquid paint with water. Try to get a strong color. Add enough water so that the paint is thin. You might want two or three colors.

2. Use a dropper bottle to paint on paper or cardboard.

3. After you have painted your artistic masterpiece, place it in the sun. The water will evaporate.

4. Give the dry painting to a friend or relative.

Salt Facts and Slogans

You used the sun's energy to evaporate salt water. This method has been used for thousands of years to take salt out of the oceans.

Salt is essential to our diet. You can get sick on hot days without it. Salt is often given to athletes.

Salt played a big part in history. It was used to preserve food and as money. Kings placed taxes on salt.

Over the years there have been many salt sayings. A good person was considered the "salt of the Earth." A lazy person was "not worth his salt."

Imagination Time
Invent your own salt-y saying. It can be serious or funny. Write your slogan in the box to the right.

22

Water Pressure

**Water
Science**

5

Squeezing Water

Air is made of molecules. There is lots of space between air molecules. You can "squeeze" air into a small space.

Water is also made of molecules. There is much less space between liquid water molecules. It is difficult to "squeeze" water into a smaller space.

Experiment

Let's "feel" the difference between air and water.

1. Find two small plastic water bottles about a quart (liter) in size with lids.
2. Fill one bottle with water. Leave the other one empty. Put the lids on tightly.
3. Squeeze the air bottle. It almost collapses in your hand. Why?
4. Squeeze the water bottle with the lid on. Is it harder to squeeze. Why?

Water bottles with lids

Water

Air

Water Pressure

Water Under Pressure

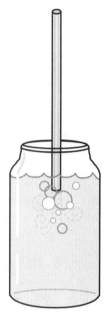

Let's imagine you are in a deep swimming pool. You dive under water. The deeper you dive the more pressure you feel on your eardrums.

The more water above you the more the pressure. Right below the water surface you hardly feel the pressure. At the pool bottom you feel the greatest pressure.

Experiment

Here is a way to "feel" water pressure.

1. Fill a tall jar with water.
2. Place the end of a drinking straw just beneath the water surface.
3. Blow into the straw to make bubbles. Is it easy to do? Why?
4. Place the end of the straw at the bottom of the jar. Blow bubbles again. Is it harder to do? Why?

Experiment

You can "feel" water pressure another way.

1. Use the same tall jar of water you used before.
2. Find a small plastic vial with a lid.
3. Push the closed vial down into the jar. The deeper you push it the more the pressure fights you.

> The deeper the water the greater the pressure. The pressure at the jar bottom resists your blowing.

24

Water Pressure

Water Pressure Waterfall

Try this experiment to see water pressure at work.

Experiment

1. Punch three small holes in a line as shown in an empty quart milk carton. Make the first hole 1" from the bottom, the second hole 3" up and the third hole 5" up. The holes should all be about the same size.

2. Do this step over a sink with someone helping you. Place your fingers tightly over all three holes and fill the carton to the top with water.

3. Uncover all three holes at the same time. Watch what happens. You may want to refill and repeat the experiment a few times so you have time to see exactly what happens.

Which hole spurted water the farthest?

Which hole spurted water the least distance?

What does this tell you about the water pressure on the bottom hole?

Be sure to get an adult to help you with this experiment!

Name _____

Water Pressure

Deep-Sea Diving

A diver deep in the ocean sees a world of beauty, but diving can be very dangerous due to water pressure. A diver at 30 feet below the water surface has double the normal pressure. At 100 feet the pressure is four times normal. That is the limit for divers without special equipment.

Imagination Time!
Imagine that you are the world's greatest deep-sea diver. You have the best equipment. You dive hundreds of feet under the ocean. Write a short story about your underwater adventures. Anything goes.

Water Has a Skin

Learning About Water's Skin

You have a skin that protects your body. Liquid water also has a skin. It forms on the surface and is made of water molecules clinging to each other.

You can see your skin. Water's skin is invisible. Insects use this skin to walk on water. The pond skater can land and walk on water.

Experiment

Let's experiment with this skin.

1. Fill a clean cereal bowl half full of water.
2. Lay a sheet of toilet tissue carefully on the water.
3. Gently place a paper clip flat on the tissue.
4. Wait a minute or two. What happened to the tissue? Why? What happened to the metal clip? Why?

The clip was held up by the water's skin. Look around the clip edges. You can see the skin bending.

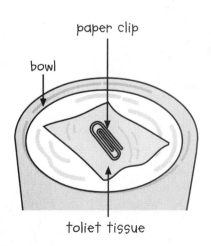

paper clip

bowl

toliet tissue

Water Has a Skin

Breaking Up the Water's Skin

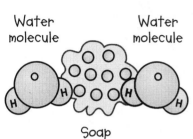

Water molecule   Water molecule

Soap

Soap can break up water's skin. It does this by moving in between the water molecules.

It is fun to see this happening.

Experiment

You'll need some sewing thread, a toothpick, some liquid soap and a bowl of water.

1. Tie the thread into a 6" loop. Place it in a bowl of clean water.

2. Use the toothpick to form the thread into an odd shape, anything but a circle.

3. Pick up a drop of liquid soap with the point of the toothpick. Touch the soapy end into the center of the thread. What happened to the thread? Why?

The soap broke up the water's skin inside the thread. The water outside the thread still has a skin. This skin pulled the thread outward.

Name _____

The Toothpick Escape

You'll need a cereal bowl, liquid soap and three clean toothpicks for this experiment.

1. Place two toothpicks in the water lined up next to each other. Use the third toothpick to line them up. Do not use your fingers.

2. Dip the third toothpick into the liquid soap. Place a drop of soap between the toothpicks on the water.

3. Describe what happened. Can you explain this in terms of the water's skin? (If you need help, read what Allie said on page 28.)

Water Has a Skin

Sailing on the Skin of Water

Make this cardboard boat that can really move.

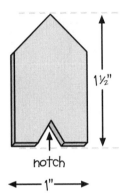

1½"

1"

notch

1. Fill a shallow pan with a thin layer of clean water. This will be your lake.
2. Cut out a 1" x 1½" cardboard boat from stiff cardboard as shown in the sketch.
3. Place the boat at one end of the "lake."
4. Dip a toothpick into liquid soap. Place the soap in the notch of the boat. Watch your boat take off.

If you want to repeat this experiment, you'll need to empty the water and replace it with clean water (with no soap in it).

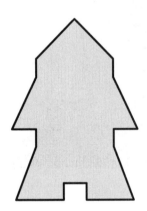

Boat Race

Challenge your friends to a boat race. Remember that you need new water for each race.

Follow these race rules:

1. Boats must be made of cardboard.
2. No boat can be over 2" long.
3. You can use any soap or detergent.
4. You can design your own shape or use one of the shapes shown on this page. Whatever shape you use, you'll need a notch at the back.

More About Water's Skin

Skin Tight Water

Water's surface acts like a skin. The skin on your stomach can bulge out if you eat too much. The skin on water can also bulge out.

Experiment

1. Fill a glass exactly to the top with water.
2. Find lots of pennies. Drop them one at a time into the glass slowly and carefully.
3. Watch the water "skin" bulge out above the brim.

Contest Fun

Challenge a friend to a water bulging contest.

1. Find two equal-sized glasses.
2. Place a dry paper towel under each.
3. Fill each glass to the brim with water.
4. Let the contest begin. The winner is the one who drops the most pennies in the water without getting the paper towel wet.

More About Water's Skin

A Lid with Holes

Here is a way to see water's skin at work.

Experiment

1. Have an adult make five large holes in the lid of a small jar. The holes should be a bit smaller than a pencil.

2. Fill the jar with water. Place the lid on it, then turn the jar upside down.

Did water come out of the lid holes? Why or why not?

Water Glue

Water molecules tend to "stick" to other molecules. Experiment to see this.

Experiment

1. Pour water into a small glass.

2. Study the surface of the water. You can see the water bulging down at the center.

3. Look where the water surface meets the glass. Why is the water higher there than in the center?

> *Water molecules are more attracted to glass than to other water molecules. The attraction is called **adhesion**.*

32

More About Water's Skin

Penny Pickup

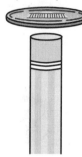

Glue a penny to the top of a pencil.

Water can stick to objects and can even be used as a glue. Here is a sticky water experiment.

Experiment

1. Glue a clean, shiny penny to the bottom of a pencil.
2. Place a second clean, shiny penny on a dry, clean surface.
3. Add two drops of water to the surface of the penny.
4. Lower the glued penny on top of the wet penny. Gently lift the pencil. Can you pick up the wet penny? You may have to try it a few times.

Water Challenge

Can you beat a friend at this game?

You'll need a small glass, a large jar and 10 pennies for each player.

1. Place the glass at the center of the bottom of the jar.
2. Fill the jar almost to the brim with water.
3. Drop the pennies from above the jar. The winner is the player who gets the most pennies in the glass.

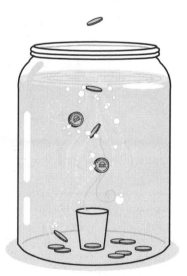

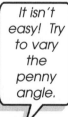

It isn't easy! Try to vary the penny angle.

Water Puzzlers

Water Science

8

5-quart jar

Pat's Pickle

3-quart jar

Puzzler 1: Measuring Four Quarts of Water

You have a three-quart jar, a five-quart jar and all the water you need. You do not have anything else—no measuring cups, no rulers and no scientific equipment.

You puzzler is to measure out exactly four quarts of water. Tell what to do, step by step, on the lines below.

Here's a helpful hint. You'll need to pour out some of the water you pour in!

Water Puzzlers

Puzzler 2: Finding Half

Quart jar

You have a quart jar. You need to measure exactly a half quart. You have only the quart jar and water—no other tools but your brain. Tell what you do, step by step, on the lines below.

Pat's Pickles

The secret is in how you hold the jar.

Puzzler 3: How Fast Can You Empty a Bottle?

To win this contest, you must be able to empty a small-necked quart (liter) plastic bottle of water faster than anyone else.

Fill the bottle to the brim with water. Then stand over a sink or go outside. Have a friend time you. Be careful and good luck. Describe what you do to be the fastest.

_____

_____

_____

_____

_____

_____

_____

_____

_____

_____

Think tornado!

Floating on Water

Floating and Sinking

Ping-Pong™ ball floats on water. Throw a rock in the water and it sinks to the bottom.

Experiment

. Put a Ping-Pong™ ball in a glass of water. It floats very high in the water.

. Push the ball under the water. It pushes back. It doesn't want to go under.

The force that pushed the ball up is called **buoyancy**. The more water you pushed aside, the more buoyancy.

Here is a way to think of buoyancy. You are floating in a swimming pool. You weigh 80 pounds. To float you must push aside 80 pounds of water. A 50-ton boat must push aside 50 tons of water to float.

Experiment

Here is a way to "feel" the buoyant force of water.

. Fill a large bowl or pan with water.

. Place some rocks in a plastic bag.

. Hold the bag a few inches above the water. It should feel heavy.

. Lower the bag into the water.

Does the bag of rocks feel lighter in the water?

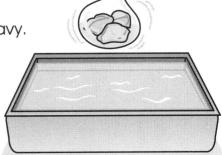

The buoyant force of the water that was pushed aside helps you. A 100-pound person floating in water would only seem to weigh 0 pounds.

Floating on Water

A Lid Boat

1. Fill a large glass bowl with water.

2. Find a metal lid about the size of a baby food jar lid.

3. Place the lid into the water sideways. Does it float or sink? Metal is heavier, so the lid should sink.

4. Gently place the lid upside down into the water. Does it float or sink? It should float because it is now shaped like a boat. It is pushing aside lots of water. This creates a buoyant force.

5. Put pennies, one at a time, in the center of your lid boat. Watch the boat sink a bit after each penny.

6. Challenge a friend to a boat sinking contest. Use the same lid each time. The winner is the one who can place the most pennies in the lid boat before it sinks.

38

Name _____

The Floating Egg

Place a fresh egg in a large glass of water. What happens? The egg is slightly heavier than the water it pushed aside.

Add a few tablespoons of salt to the water. Carefully stir the salt into the water until it dissolves.

Keep adding salt and stirring until the egg floats to the top. Why does this make the egg float?

Salt water is "heavier" than pure water. The heavier salt water has more buoyancy. Remember that buoyancy is an upward force that helps things float.

Dense Water

Feathers are light. Steel is heavy.

Scientists measure heaviness with a term called **density**. Density is given as a number that compares how heavy things are. (See page 41.)

Water is the standard for density. It is number 1 on the density scale. Anything over 1 will sink in water. Anything under 1 will float in water.

Density Quiz

Study the density table on page 41. Then answer these questions.

1. Name five items that will float in water. _____

   _____

   _____

2. Name five items that will sink in water. _____

   _____

   _____

3. What is the lightest item on the density table? _____

4. What is the heaviest item on the table? _____

5. Would gasoline float or sink in water? _____

6. What is the lightest metal on the table? _____

Density Table

(All density numbers compared to water's density of 1.)

Solids	Metals	Liquids
Bone. 2	Aluminum. 2.7	Pure Water 1
Brick. 1.8	Copper. 8.9	Sea Water 1.03
Cork. 0.2	Gold 19.3	Alcohol. 0.8
Ice 0.92	Iron 7.8	Glycerine 1.3
Marble 2.7	Lead 11.3	Milk 1.03
Paraffin 0.9	Silver 10.5	Turpentine 0.9
Rubber 1.2		Mercury 13.6
Bamboo 0.3		Gasoline 0.7
Oak Wood 0.7		
Pine Wood 0.6		

Name _____

Research Time

A man named Archimedes discovered the laws of **buoyancy**. He lived in Greece over 2000 years ago. His discovery involved a fake gold crown. Look him up and write about his discoveries below.

_____

_____

_____

_____

_____

_____

Buoyancy has meanings other than floating. Look up these other meanings in a dictionary. Also look up **buoy**. Write your findings below.

_____

_____

_____

_____

42

Water and Your Body

Why Your Body Needs Water

Your body is 66% water. The blood that flows through you is 90% water. Your bones look dry, but they are 20% water.

You should drink six to eight glasses of water a day to replace the water your body loses through sweat and urine.

Even your breath gives off water. Here is how to see your exhaled water.

Experiment

1. Place a small mirror in the refrigerator for 10 minutes.

2. Breathe on the mirror.

What do you see on the mirror?

The air in your breath is moist and warm. The cold mirror causes it to condense into water that you can see.

43

Water and Your Body

Cooling Water

Your body tries to keep a normal temperature of 98.6° Fahrenheit. On hot days you must sweat to keep that temperature.

Experiment

Try this cooling experiment.

1. Place some water on your wrist.
2. Wave your hand around.

How did your wrist feel?

Finish this sentence to explain what happened.

As water evaporates it _____ your body.

Here is another body cooling experiment.

Experiment

1. Find a clear plastic bag and some tape.
2. Place the bag over your hand. Tape it loosely as shown.
3. Wait 10 minutes.

What do you see forming inside the bag?

How did this water get out of your body?

Water moving through your skin cools you. It also eliminates waste.

Water and Your Body

Water and Food

Some water you drink as liquids. Some water you get in solid foods. An egg is 75% water. An apple is 85% water. Lettuce is 96% water.

Experiment

Let's force water out of a solid food.

1. Place some dry lima beans in an old pan.
2. Have an adult heat the pan on a stove.

   What do you see coming off the lima beans?

   Water is also needed to digest food. The watery saliva in your mouth starts digesting starchy foods.

Caution!
Always have an adult help you when working on the stove.

Experiment

Let's put saliva to work.

1. Try to find an unsalted cracker. (A salted cracker will work if you can't find an unsalted one.) Crackers mainly contain starch.
2. Chew the cracker but do not swallow it. Let as much of your saliva as possible mix with the cracker.
3. Describe how the cracker tastes.

It should taste sweet. Saliva changes starch to sugar.

Name _____

Water and Your Senses

It is hard to judge temperature without a thermometer. Your body's sense of temperature is not accurate.

Here is a way to fool your heat sense. Try this on yourself and others.

Experiment

1. Find three equal-sized bowls.

2. Fill one bowl with water and place it in the refrigerator for 10 minutes.

3. After 10 minutes fill another bowl with very warm water.

4. Fill the third bowl with room temperature water.

5. Place one hand into the warm water.

6. Place the other hand into the cold water. Leave them there for a fu minute.

7. Now quickly place both hands in the room temperature water.

How did the cold hand feel?

How did the warm hand feel?

Your sense of heat depends on what you are used to.

Do-It-Yourself Experiments

1. Solid food contains some water. Bread is about 25% water. Plan an exper iment to prove that bread has water.

2. Dogs cool off through their tongues. Observe how dogs do this.

Warm water   Normal water   Cold water

Water and Plants

Plants Need Water

Many plants are 90% water. They actually need and use more water than animals.

Plants need water to dissolve minerals in the soil. Water carries these minerals up to the leaves.

Plants need water to move food made in leaves back to the roots.

Plant cells are packed with water. This helps them stay rigid.

Here is an experiment that shows how water moves up in a plant.

Experiment

1. Cut a fresh stalk of celery, with a clean cut near the bottom.
2. Fill a tall glass half full of water.
3. Add lots of red vegetable dye to the water.
4. Place the celery in the water. Store it in a dark area overnight.
5. Look at the celery stalk. Describe what you see. Which way does water flow in a plant?

_____

_____

_____

_____

_____

Water and Plants

Plant Perspiration

You perspire and so do plants. Plant "perspira-tion" is called **transpiration**. An elm tree can transpire 100 gallons a day.

Study the transpiration diagram. Water is pulled up by the roots and carried to the leaves.

Leaves have small open-ings like your skin pores. The water escapes through the leaves into the air.

You can substitute a houseplant if it is more convenient

Experiment

Let's trap transpired water in a clear plastic bag.

1. Find a bush or low tree around your school or home in a sunny area.

2. Tie a plastic bag over a branch of leaves as shown.

3. Look at the bag in a few hours.

   What do you see inside the bag?

   Where did this water come from?

4. Try to explain plant transpiration in your own words below.

_____

_____

_____

_____

_____

Water and Plants

Seeds Need Water

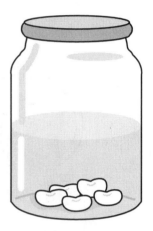

1. Find five large dried lima beans. Feel them. How do they feel?

2. Line up the five beans along a ruler as shown. Measure their total length and write it here.

   Length of five dry beans = _____ inches

3. Place all five beans in a covered jar half full of water.

4. Store them in a warm, dark place overnight.

5. Feel the beans. Are they still hard and dry? What was absorbed into the beans? What do all seeds need to start growing? Have the beans grown in size? Line them up along a ruler to measure all five and write their length here.

   Length of five soaked beans = _____ inches

Don't throw away the soaked beans. You will need them again!

A Lima Bean Growing Contest

Why not try to grow the soaked lima beans from the experiment on page 49? Compete with your friends to see who can grow the tallest bean plant in 10 days. You can only plant five beans.

Here are some hints to help you become a super bean farmer.

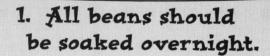

1. All beans should be soaked overnight.

2. Use a different container for each of your five beans.

3. Use loose soil, potting mixtures or sawdust.

4. Place the beans about one inch under the soil.

5. Keep the soil damp but not flooded.

6. Store containers in a warm dark place until they sprout. Then move them into the sun.

7. Give your bean plants tender loving care.

Name _____

Key Word Review

Use key words from the box to complete the statements.

seeds	roots	transpiration
water	leaves	upward

1. Plants use more _____ than animals.

2. Plants take in water through their _____.

3. Plants give off water through their _____.

4. Plant perspiration is called _____.

5. _____ must take in water before they can grow.

6. Water flows _____ in plants.

The Water Cycle

Water Goes Around and Around

Water is everywhere. It is snow on the tops of mountains. It is clouds in the sky. Water is the rain that falls from clouds.

Water does not stay in one place. It moves around the Earth in a **water cycle**.

Study the water cycle chart to see how water moves around.

Clouds are made of water. As clouds cool, water falls to Earth as rain or snow.

Rain falls on land and sea. Water on land flows in rivers back to the sea.

The sun heats the Earth. Water evaporates and rises to form clouds.

The water cycle never stops. The water in a cloud may come out of your faucet next week. Dew forms on grass in the morning. The noon sun evaporates the dew back into the sky.

Name _____

A Water Cycle Experiment

1. Find a clear plastic box with a lid.
2. Pour a small glass of water into the box.
3. Add enough vegetable dye to give the water a dark color.
4. Place the lid on the box and put it in bright sunlight.
5. Wait 10 to 20 minutes.

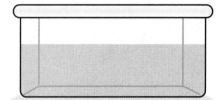

What do you see forming on the sides and lid of the box?

What provided the energy to evaporate the water?

Did the dye evaporate with the water?

Name _____

The Story of Water

There is only so much water on Earth. It is recycled constantly. The raindrop that hits your head may have hit a dinosaur years ago.

Imagination Time!
Make up a story about the adventures of a raindrop. You can go back a thousand or a hundred or a million years. Your story may involve famous people or your own ancestors.

_____

_____

_____

_____

_____

_____

_____

_____

_____

_____

_____

_____

_____

_____

_____

54

Water Cycle Crossword Puzzle

All the words in this puzzle involve the water cycle.

Down

1. Ten-letter word. What the sun does to water.
2. Five-letter word. This can be a solid, liquid or gas.
4. Six letters. Water that is not a solid or a gas.

Across

3. Six letters. Where most of the Earth's water is found.
5. Four letters. Water falling from clouds.
6. Four letters. Found on the tops of mountains.
7. Three letters. Solid form of water.

Water Science 13

Protecting and Saving Water

Water in Our Life

We drink water, we swim in water, we water our plants, we wash our clothes, we flush our toilets.

It is hard to imagine a world without water.

Most of the time our water is fresh and pure. The water that you drink is tested constantly for safety. This is not true for some of the six billion people on Earth. Their water may be polluted.

How does water get polluted? People pollute. Farms pollute with animal waste and pesticides. Barges or tankers may spill oil into oceans or rivers. Some factories give off harmful chemicals. Some of these chemicals go into the air and return as acid rain.

Protecting and Saving Water

Fighting Water Pollution

Nature does a good job of fighting water pollution. Water evaporates from spoiled water and leaves the pollutants behind. Only pure water reaches the clouds and becomes rain.

Gravity also helps make water pure. Polluted water filters down through beds of gravel and gets cleaner.

Here is a way to show how gravity can help clear water.

Experiment

1. Fill a tall jar with a tight lid $3/4$ full of water.

2. Add about three tablespoons of dirt.

3. Put the lid on and shake the jar vigorously. You now have polluted water.

4. Describe how the water looks. Would you drink it?

5. Let the water sit for 15 minutes.

What part of the water is clearest?

Where is most of the dirt? Why?

Gravity pulled much of the dirt down. The water at the top could be made even cleaner by filtering it through a cloth. Chemicals could be added to kill germs.

Protecting and Saving Water

Conserving Water

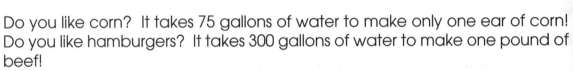

We use a lot of water. A shower can take 20 gallons. A toilet flush can be two to four gallons.

Do you like corn? It takes 75 gallons of water to make only one ear of corn! Do you like hamburgers? It takes 300 gallons of water to make one pound of beef!

There are many ways you can save water. You can start by thinking of ways to save water at home. Ask your parents to help. List your water-saving ideas.

Saving water in the kitchen

1._____

2._____

3._____

4._____

Saving water in the garden

1._____

2._____

3._____

4._____

Saving water in the bathroom

1._____

2._____

3._____

4._____

Saving water at school

1._____

2._____

3._____

4._____

Saving water in the laundry room

1._____

2._____

3._____

4._____

Name _____

"Save the Water" Poster

A good poster can make people think about saving water. Do your part to conserve water by creating a poster with a valuable message. Follow these guidelines.

The poster should be about conserving water.

Emphasize saving water at home or at school.

The poster should have a slogan as well as a drawing.

Sketch your poster idea below before you put it on poster board.

Display your completed poster in a public place.

Review Scramble

The sentences below describe words used in this lesson.
The words are mixed up. Can you unscramble them?

1.   Used to kill germs found in polluted water.

   MESCHILAC

   _____

2.   A water pollutant spilled from ocean tankers.

   LOI

   _____

3.   Rain that contains pollutants.

   DACI

   _____

4.   Pollutant that runs off farms.

   PICIDEEST

   _____

Here's a bonus word:
It helps make water pure.
ITAGYVR

_____

Frozen Water

Water Science

14

Oxygen atom

Hydrogen atoms

Explaining Ice

Water and ice are made of the same molecule. Both have two atoms of hydrogen and one atom of oxygen. The formula is H_2O.

The only difference between water and ice is molecular motion. Ice molecules move slower than water molecules.

Let's observe an ice cube. Place one in a glass of water.

Does the ice cube float or sink? If it floats, it must be lighter than water.

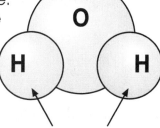

Only 10% of an ice cube is above the water. The rest is below the water surface.

Icebergs are giant ice cubes. They come from glacier ice sheets that fall into the ocean.

Suppose you find a small iceberg that sticks out 10 feet above the water.

How much ice is below the water? _____

Icebergs can be dangerous to ships. It was an iceberg that sank the *Titanic*.

Freezing Water Experiment

1. Fill a small plastic water bottle to the top with water.
2. Place it in the freezer without a cap.
3. Wait 24 hours.
4. Look at the frozen water bottle. Describe how it looks.

Look closely at the bottle top. Has the ice expanded?

_____

_____

Save the frozen bottle for the experiment on page 63!

Most things in the world shrink when frozen. Water is the only substance that expands when frozen.

Frozen Water

Frozen Bottle Challenge

How long can you keep the bottle of ice from the experiment on page 62 frozen? Compete with your friends.

There is only one rule. You can't use a refrigerator. Almost anything else goes. Pack the bottle any way you wish to keep the ice from melting.

The contest is over in 24 hours. The largest remaining ice chunk wins.

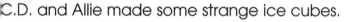

Ice Cube Fun

C.D. and Allie made some strange ice cubes.

- A colored ice cube
- A multicolored ice cube
- A round ice cube
- A domino-shaped ice cube
- An ice cube with a hole in the center

Can you make them, too?
Be ready to explain how you made each one.

Answer Key

Review Quiz, page 8

1. ice
2. steam
3. 10
4. 3%
5. Answers will vary.

Key Word Review, page 13

1. moving
2. fast
3. slow
4. shape
5. container
6. escape

Puzzler 1, page 34

Measuring Four Quarts of Water
Fill the three-quart jar completely with water. Pour the three quarts into the five-quart jar. Refill the three-quart jar. Use it to fill the five quart jar to the top. This will leave one quart of water in the three-quart jar. Pour all the water out of the five-quart jar. Pour the one quart left in the three-quart jar into the five-quart jar. Fill the three-quart jar with water. Add the three quarts to the one quart. You now have four quarts measured.

Puzzler 2, page 35

Finding Half
Add water to the jar so it is obviously over half full. Hold the jar over a sink. Tilt the jar to slowly pour the water out. Stop pouring when the water surface touches both the top of the jar and the point where the side and bottom join. At this point the jar is half full.

Puzzler 3, page 36

How Fast Can You Empty a Bottle?
Air pressure is working against you in this puzzler, keeping the water in the bottle. You must get air inside the jar to force the water out. Hold the jar firmly with two hands over a sink. Rotate it rapidly to form a tornado-like funnel inside the jar. Stop rotating and let the air come in and push the water out.

Density Quiz, page 40

1. alcohol, turpentine, gasoline, cork, paraffin, bamboo, oak wood, pine wood, ice
2. bone, brick, marble, rubber, aluminum, copper, gold, iron, lead, silver, sea water, glycerine, milk, mercury
3. cork
4. gold
5. float
6. aluminum

Key Word Review, page 51

1. water
2. roots
3. leaves
4. transpiration
5. seeds
6. upward

Water Cycle Crossword Puzzle, page 55

Review Scramble, page 60

1. chemicals
2. oil
3. acid
4. pesticide
Bonus: gravity